Oxford University Press, Walton Street, Oxford OX2 6DP
Oxford New York Toronto
Delhi Bombay Calcutta Madras Karachi
Petaling Jaya Singapore Hong Kong Tokyo
Nairobi Dar es Salaam Cape Town
Melbourne Auckland

and associated companies in
Beirut Berlin Ibadan Nicosia

Oxford is a trade mark of Oxford University Press

© William Stobbs 1987

British Library Cataloguing in Publication Data
Stobbs, William
    A frog he would a-wooing go
    I. Title
    389'.8   PZ8.3

    ISBN 0 19 279848 0

Typeset by PGT Graphic Design, Oxford
Printed in Hong Kong

A frog he would a-wooing go

WILLIAM STOBBS

Oxford University Press

A frog he would a-wooing go,
   Heigh ho! says Rowley,
Whether his mother would let him or no.
   With a rowley, powley, gammon and spinach,
   Heigh ho! says Anthony Rowley.

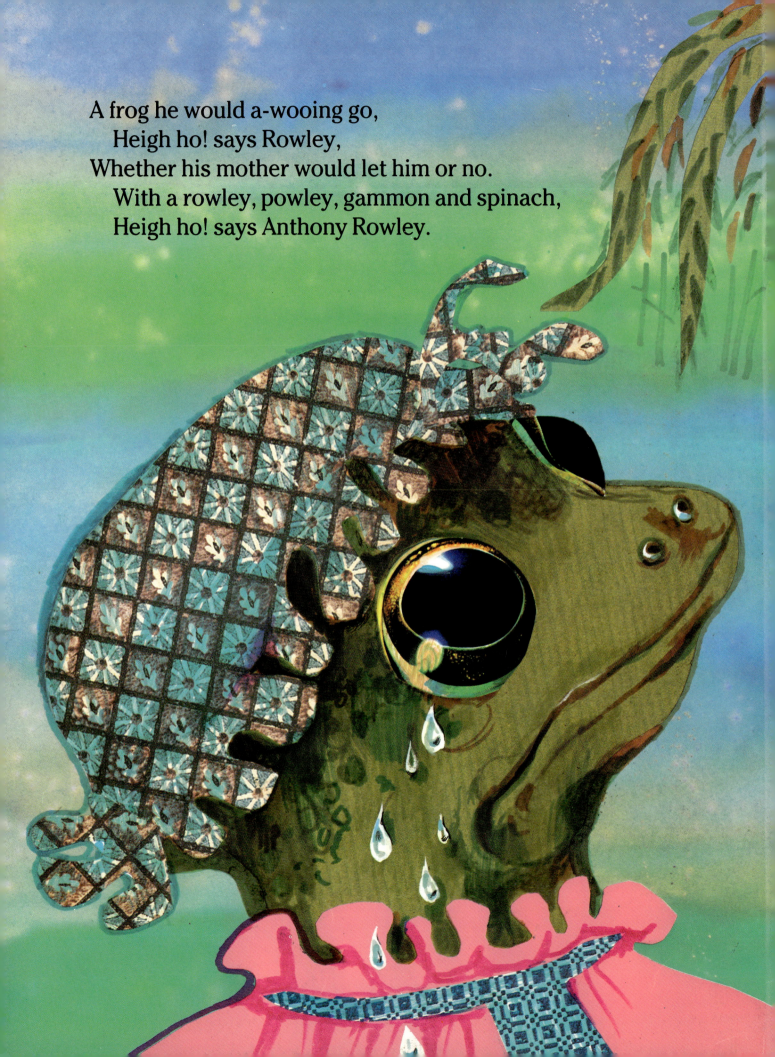

So off he set with his best straw hat,
 Heigh ho! says Rowley,
And on the road he met with a rat.
 With a rowley, powley, gammon and spinach,
 Heigh ho! says Anthony Rowley.

Pray, Mister Rat, will you go with me?
  Heigh ho! says Rowley,
Kind Mistress Mousey for to see?
  With a rowley, powley, gammon and spinach,
  Heigh ho! says Anthony Rowley.

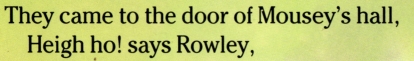

They came to the door of Mousey's hall,
  Heigh ho! says Rowley,
They gave a loud knock, and they gave a loud call.
  With a rowley, powley, gammon and spinach,
  Heigh ho! says Anthony Rowley.

Missie Mousey

Pray, Mistress Mouse, are you within?
　　Heigh ho! says Rowley,
Oh yes, kind sirs, I'm sitting to spin.
　　With a rowley, powley, gammon and spinach,
　　Heigh ho! says Anthony Rowley.

Pray, Mistress Mouse, will you give us some beer?
　　Heigh ho! says Rowley,
For Froggy and I are fond of good cheer.
　　With a rowley, powley, gammon and spinach,
　　Heigh ho! says Anthony Rowley.

Pray, Mister Frog, will you give us a song?
    Heigh ho! says Rowley,
Let it be something that's not very long.
    With a rowley, powley, gammon and spinach,
    Heigh ho! says Anthony Rowley.

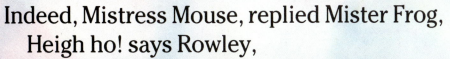

Indeed, Mistress Mouse, replied Mister Frog,
   Heigh ho! says Rowley,
A cold has made me as hoarse as a dog.
   With a rowley, powley, gammon and spinach,
   Heigh ho! says Anthony Rowley.

Since you've got a cold, Miss Mousey said,
  Heigh ho! says Rowley,
I'll sing you a song that I have just made.
  With a rowley, powley, gammon and spinach,
  Heigh ho! says Anthony Rowley.

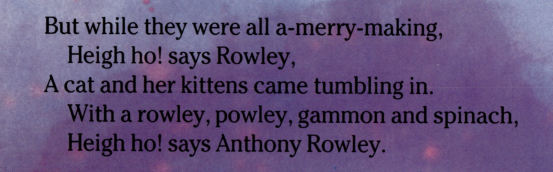

But while they were all a-merry-making,
　　Heigh ho! says Rowley,
A cat and her kittens came tumbling in.
　　With a rowley, powley, gammon and spinach,
　　Heigh ho! says Anthony Rowley.

The cat she seized the rat by the crown,
  Heigh ho! says Rowley,
The kittens they pulled the little mouse down.
  With a rowley, powley, gammon and spinach,
  Heigh ho! says Anthony Rowley.

This put Mister Frog in a terrible fright,
    Heigh ho! says Rowley,
He took up his hat and he wished them good-night.
    With a rowley, powley, gammon and spinach,
    Heigh ho! says Anthony Rowley.

But as Froggy was crossing over a brook,
  Heigh ho! says Rowley,
A lily-white duck came and gobbled him up.
  With a rowley, powley, gammon and spinach,
  Heigh ho! says Anthony Rowley.

So there was an end of one, two, three,
  Heigh ho! says Rowley,
The rat, the mouse, and the little frog-ee.
  With a rowley, powley, gammon and spinach,
  Heigh ho! says Anthony Rowley.